MW01690404

# God With Us

## THE STORY OF THE MESSIAH

PRESENTED TO

BY

DATE

Lifeway Press®
Brentwood, Tennessee

ISBN 978-1-0877-8475-5
Item 005842347
Dewey Decimal Classification Number: 242
Subject Heading: DEVOTIONAL LITERATURE / BIBLE STUDY AND TEACHING / GOD

Printed in the United States of America.

Student Ministry Publishing
Lifeway Resources
200 Powell Place, Suite 100
Brentwood, TN 37027

We believe that the Bible has God for its author; salvation for its end; truth, without any mixture of error, for its matter; and that all Scripture is totally true and trustworthy. To review Lifeway's doctrinal guideline, please visit www.lifeway.com/doctrinalguideline.



# publishing team

*Director, Student Ministry*
Ben Trueblood

*Manager, Student Publishing*
Karen Daniel

*Writer*
Jay Watson

*Content Editor*
Kyle Wiltshire

*Production Editor*
April-Lyn Caouette

*Graphic Designers*
Shiloh Stufflebeam
Grace Morgan

# Table of Contents

# *Intro*

It comes around once a year, and it's one of the most anticipated days for much of the world. In fact, you're probably counting down the days to this special occasion right now. Of course I'm talking about Christmas! I'm sure you know the basics of what it's all about—Mary, Joseph, baby Jesus, some shepherds, a star, angels, an evil king, some wise men. But there's so much more to it than that. The story of Christmas actually began thousands of years earlier.

Believe it or not, the entire Bible was building to that special day. Every moment in the Old Testament was like a stepping stone toward it. Then, at just the right time, God sent Jesus—the Messiah—into the world, to be carried by a special teenage girl named Mary. The title *Messiah* means "promised deliverer." Jesus is the promised One to whom the entire Old Testament was pointing, and He is the subject of the entire New Testament. He came to deliver Israel and the world from sin, shame, and darkness.

Where do you fit into this wonderful story? Over the next thirty days you will hear the amazing, true story of the Messiah and have the opportunity to place your hope in Him. If you already are a Christian, then you have been empowered by the Holy Spirit, who lives in you. You have the ability to look back at the Old and New Testaments together to see the beauty of God's faithful goodness. With a clear mind, an open heart, and a faith that is growing in you right now, you can live your life for the God of the universe. God so loved the world that He gave His only Son, Jesus: God with us.

# Getting Started

This devotional contains thirty days of content, broken down into sections. Each day is divided into three elements—**discover**, **delight**, and **display**—to help you grow in your faith and guide your time in God's Word.

## DISCOVER

This section helps you examine the passage in light of who God is and determine what it says about your identity in relationship to Him. Included here is the daily Scripture reading and key verses, along with illustrations and commentary to guide you as you learn more about God's Word.

## DELIGHT

In this section, you'll be challenged by questions and activities that help you see how God is alive and active in every detail of His Word and in your life.

## DISPLAY

Here's where you take action. This section calls you to apply what you've learned through each day.

**Each day also includes a prayer activity at the conclusion of the devotion.**

**Throughout the devotional, you'll also find extra items to help you connect with the topic personally, such as Scripture memory verses and interactive articles.**

Section 1

# Prophecies of the Messiah

**Repeatedly throughout the Old Testament, humans chose to sin and reject God while God chose to be faithful. God empowered prophets to share His message, and those prophets spoke truth to Israel. God's words pointed to a Messiah who would offer hope. Many of the prophecies were not clear until after Jesus ascended to heaven. Now we can very clearly see God's plan all along.**

## DAY 1

# Next Door Neighbor

READ JOHN 1:1-18.

*In the beginning was the Word, and the Word was with God, and the Word was God. He was with God in the beginning.*
*— John 1:1-2*

## DISCOVER

What is the earliest memory you have? Is it a place, person, or moment? Do you remember how old you were or who else was there? It's strange to think about, but even though you can't remember it, you existed before your first memory of being alive. There is evidence of the day you were born and the name you were given. There were witnesses, a birth certificate, and maybe even pictures to prove it. I don't think anyone could ever disagree with the idea that you existed before you were old enough to have memory of it.

One of the names Jesus has in Scripture is "the Word." John wrote that Jesus was—that is, He already existed—at the beginning of all creation. God wasn't created; the Bible tells us that He was, is, and always will be. In the book of Genesis, God promised a Savior. Thousands of years later, a baby was born. Angels proclaimed this birth to shepherds and told them to check the manger in Bethlehem to see for themselves.

How are you and I supposed to believe something like this when we didn't experience it? God's Word is consistent. Over thousands of years, it reveals to us a God who loves, shows mercy, and always keeps His promises. There is evidence we can trust.

There will be times when we have doubts. Sometimes this has to do with what we've experienced and our memories of the past. But God's Word reminds us that God not only loves us right now—He always has and He always will. His Word is evidence of things that are sometimes difficult to understand.

## DELIGHT

**How many different names is Jesus called in these verses? How do they help you understand who Jesus is?**

**How do these few verses describe the gospel—or the good news—of Jesus Christ to you?**

**John essentially described the God of the universe as becoming a next door neighbor. How does Jesus's existence on earth reveal God's love for you personally?**

## DISPLAY

Go find a few people who were alive and around before the earliest memories you have of yourself. Ask them what you were like as a baby and what they remember. Find out what they were doing and if they remember anything interesting. Tell them about your first memories and see if your memories match up with how they remember things.

Go back to your room or someplace private, and prayerfully consider how all these things line up with the truth you know about yourself and God. Jot down a few notes on how God was faithful to you even before you were old enough to remember. Take some time to consider the greatness of God in all of these events in your life.

**Talk with God about the things you learned from John 1:1-18. Call Him the names that John used in Scripture. Ask God to shine His truth in the dark places in your life. Ask Him to give you faith to trust things about Him that sometimes seem too hard to understand.**

DAY 2

# The Plan

READ GENESIS 3.

*I will put hostility between you and the woman, and between your offspring and her offspring. He will strike your head, and you will strike his heel.*
*— Genesis 3:15*

## DISCOVER

It is possible you've heard this story growing up: Adam and Eve experienced a perfect relationship with God in the garden of Eden. They were tempted to eat the fruit that they thought would allow them to know everything God knew, and that temptation proved to be too much. Adam ate the fruit then tried to blame Eve for it. This one moment introduced sin and death into a previously perfect world.

Have you ever read Genesis 3:15 before today? God made a promise that the serpent would be crushed and defeated. The truth of this verse is expressed again in Romans 16:20, Hebrews 2:14, and Revelation 20:1-3,10. This is God's first promise to redeem the world from the clutches of sin and evil.

If you haven't before, I hope you realize today that God's plan for salvation through Jesus Christ has been in motion since the very beginning. In fact, everything that we read in the Old Testament points us to God's plan for our redemption.

God's Word is as powerful today as it ever has been. His truth is for you. Sin and shame have been around since this moment in the garden, but God's love and forgiveness have been consistently present, from the beginning of time right up to today. He loves you, and He proves this love by keeping His promises. Jesus's life ministry, death, and resurrection defeated sin and death. God also kept His promise to that serpent: when Jesus died on the cross, Satan was defeated. God is always and forever faithful.

## DELIGHT

**After reading Genesis 3, what specifically did Adam and Eve do wrong? What were the consequences of their sin?**

**Read the passages mentioned before (Rom. 16:20; Heb. 2:14; Rev. 20:1-3,10). How has God kept the promise of Genesis 3:15? How will He ultimately fulfill it?**

## DISPLAY

In the space provided for you below, write out two or three promises that you didn't keep recently. Maybe you did the thing you told your parents you wouldn't do, or maybe you shared a secret you were asked to keep private. Take your time and think about ways you don't keep your word from time to time. Now, next to this, write out all the ways you have known God to keep His promises. Think about God's faithfulness compared to your own.

| Promises I Didn't Keep | Promises God Has Kept |
| --- | --- |
| | |

**Your prayer today should revolve around your sin versus God's faithfulness. Tell Him all the ways you fall short and all the ways you see Him keeping His promises to you. Ask God to help you to be honest with yourself and others, and ask Him to help you walk in His grace and forgiveness. Finally ask Him to help you be more like Jesus in your words and deeds.**

## DAY 3

# #blessed

READ GENESIS 12:1-9.

*"I will make you into a great nation, I will bless you, I will make your name great, and you will be a blessing. I will bless those who bless you, I will curse anyone who treats you with contempt, and all the peoples on earth will be blessed through you."*
*— Genesis 12:2-3*

## DISCOVER

Did you know Abraham (also called Abram) worshiped other gods—false gods—before God spoke to him? Abraham was literally an idol worshiper. He was just a guy, living with his family. He had normal struggles and in no way had the outward appearance of man who would one day be the father to an entire nation.

Then God spoke to Abraham, and his life was changed forever. Abraham didn't deserve it. He wasn't especially good or different. The only significant thing that could be said about Abraham was the response he made to God: he acted in faith. God said go, and Abraham went.

Why did God do this thing for Abraham? The same reason He did it for Israel and continues to show us blessing. He is showing His perfect love and complete faithfulness to a world that doesn't deserve it. That is the grace of God. Through Abraham, God displayed that nothing is impossible for Him. He can take an old married couple like Abraham and Sarah and give them a child. From this blessing would come God's promise of a nation. From this nation would come God's promised Messiah. And the Messiah would bless all the peoples of the earth. Jesus was sent as a fulfillment of God's promise to save anyone who believes.

## DELIGHT

**Abraham obeyed God when God called him. In what areas of your life are you struggling to obey God? What needs to happen for you to be obedient like Abraham?**

**Was Abraham really a blessing to all people on earth? How is it possible for him to bless everyone?**

## DISPLAY

Spend some time listening for God's voice in your prayer time. Don't expect an audible noise. Instead, take some time, read over this passage and what you have learned, then ask God to speak to you from His truth. Be still before God and listen. See where your mind goes and whether or not it lines up with His Word. This may feel uncomfortable at first—that's okay. Take your time and begin the practice of listening for God to speak to you. If what you hear is truly from the Holy Spirit, it will match what God says in Scripture. The God of the universe wants to have a relationship with you. Take time to listen.

**Read today's passage again. Ask God to reveal His truth to you. Listen.**

**This is the difficult part: Will you respond and obey the way Abraham did?**

## DAY 4

# *Altar Call*

READ GENESIS 22:1-19.

*Abraham looked up and saw a ram caught in the thicket by its horns. So Abraham went and took the ram and offered it as a burnt offering in place of his son.*
*— Genesis 22:13*

## DISCOVER

Previously, Abraham heard God's call and responded in obedience. Then between Genesis chapters 12 and 22, a lot of life happened. Abraham and Sarah became parents in their old age to a boy named Isaac, and Isaac became the seed of hope from whom a nation would be born. Can you imagine what that was like? A voice telling Abraham that he would be the father of a nation is one thing, but to have that voice keep His promise had to be mind blowing.

Can you imagine the way Sarah must have looked at Isaac? This child was beloved and celebrated at every turn. That is what makes this passage so shocking to consider. The same God who asked Abraham to follow Him was now asking Abraham to offer up his son as a sacrifice. Why did God do this?

Abraham was being asked to display His faith in the God of the universe. He knew God was good and would provide, so he did exactly what God asked him to do. God stepped in and provided a perfect replacement sacrifice at the right moment.

Genesis 22 clearly points us to the cross and Jesus. Do you see God pointing to His plan of salvation all the way back in the time of Abraham? A perfect sacrifice, standing in the place for another, given as an offering to God. Just as God provided for Abraham, He provided Jesus for us.

## DELIGHT

**Take a moment and review the specific details of how Abraham was obedient to God's request. Where are the times you see Abraham's faith on display?**

**It seemed like God had asked Abraham to do the unthinkable, but in reality, God was testing Abraham's faith. When has God tested your faith in unexpected ways? What was the outcome?**

## DISPLAY

Pretend that your bed is an altar. In its simplest form, an altar is a place where you offer up your life to God. Think about your life and the things that, at times, you might selfishly consider more valuable than your relationship with God. Either physically or with some sort of physical representation, take the things you cherish most and place them on your bed. Offer these things to Him as a sacrifice.

**Spend time asking God to help you trust Him more than these cherished things. An example of what you can pray: "God, I want to worship only You. I give these things, these fears, these concerns to You. I give control of my life to You. Help me to listen to You and live for You. Amen."**

## DAY 5

# The Staff of Judah

READ GENESIS 49:8-14.

*The scepter will not depart from Judah or the staff from between his feet until he whose right it is comes and the obedience of the peoples belongs to him.*
*— Genesis 49:10*

## DISCOVER

How do you go from one old man to an entire nation? This is probably what Abraham wondered but never doubted. Abraham had Isaac. Isaac had Jacob. Jacob had a bunch of kids. Those sons became the beginnings of a civilization. The Hebrews (Abraham's people) eventually made their way to Egypt and flourished to the point that over the course of several hundred years they became a large nation.

As Jacob was near death, he gave out blessings and directions from God. One of these blessings pointed to a path from which a Messiah would arise. From the house of Judah would come forth a "ruler."

It is important to understand this history because the Bible is explaining how Abraham went from being one old man with one son to becoming a nation that shows the world the love of God. He would bless the world through the Hebrews from the lineage of Judah.

If you read Genesis 38, you'll find out that Judah wasn't always a good guy. In fact, he was despicable at times. However, Judah chose a path of forgiveness and making things right when he was found out. God used Judah's poor choices for redemption. The path from Abraham to Jesus is filled with people who made poor choices. This is the beautiful thing about God's plan. Jesus is the answer to sin and shame. We are called to obey Christ because of what He has done.

## DELIGHT

**When have you seen God redeem and use a person with a checkered past like Judah?**

**Why is it so important to be reminded that God keeps His promises?**

## DISPLAY

See how far back you can trace your spiritual lineage. Start with the person who led you to Christ. Ask that person who led him or her to Christ. Keep going as far back as you can. Write down the names and trace the hand of God's grace in your life.

**Take a moment and thank God for what He has done, what He is doing, and what He will do.**

**An example: "God, thank You for how You brought me to Jesus. Thank You for giving others the boldness to share Your good news. Help me to do that for other people. Amen."**

## DAY 6

# *How to Live*

READ DEUTERONOMY 18:9-22.

*"The LORD your God will raise up for you a prophet like me from among your own brothers. You must listen to him."*
*— Deuteronomy 18:15*

## DISCOVER

A nation of people from Abraham grew and were enslaved by the nation Egypt, where they lived at the time (see Ex. 1). After God delivered the Israelites from slavery in Egypt, there needed to be laws to guide them. God used Moses to speak to His people. God gave Moses the Ten Commandments and the Law designed to set Israel apart from all other nations.

The reason God mentioned such crazy scenarios as parents burning their children as offerings, sorcery, fortunes, and other horrible things was that the people of other nations were doing those things. He wanted Israel to be different. They were to only worship the one true God. Living differently meant setting up clear laws and directions for His people.

At this time, God chose to lead His people through not kings but prophets who would speak God's word to the people. These prophets had the job of listening to God and sharing God's truth as well as the promises He would make. These promises would be ways that His people and the world would see His faithfulness. This passage is a prophecy that not only speaks about their immediate future but also predicts the greatest prophet—Jesus.

God doesn't call us to a mysterious life that we need to discover. God clearly explains His will and His ways through His Word and through the ultimate fulfillment of His plan—Jesus Christ. Jesus's life, ministry, teachings, death, and resurrection help us to know how we are called to live.

## DELIGHT

**Why do you think God chose prophets at this stage of the story to lead His people instead of kings, governments, or other groups of people?**

**How can you discern whether or not teaching is true and accurate?**

## DISPLAY

Write down five laws or commands that you think come directly from God and His Word. Now, go and try to find the exact verses where they appear in Scripture. Compare what you thought God's Word said with what God actually says in His Word. What were the differences? It is easy to get misled if you don't know how to read Scripture or what it says.

Finally, read Matthew 22:37-40. Think about how all of the laws and commands you just looked up fit within these words from Jesus.

**Today's prayer should focus on knowing and trusting God's Word. Ask God to help you to grow in your knowledge of what the Bible says and how you are supposed to live. Ask God to give you an attitude of excitement about reading Scripture. Finally, ask God to give you strength to obey what He calls you to do.**

*Memory Verse*

**In the beginning was**

***the Word,***

**and the Word was**

***with God,***

**and the Word**

***was God.***

**He was with God in the**

***beginning.***

**John 1:1-2**

DAY 7

# Promise Keeper

READ 2 SAMUEL 7.

*When your time comes and you rest with your ancestors, I will raise up after you your descendant, who will come from your body, and I will establish his kingdom. He is the one who will build a house for my name, and I will establish the throne of his kingdom forever.*
*— 2 Samuel 7:12-13*

## DISCOVER

Abraham had enough faith to leave his old way of life and take his family on a journey of promise. Moses led the people of Israel out of captivity and created a new nation under God. David was called a man after God's own heart (see 1 Sam. 13:14).

David was far from perfect; he made extremely human and sinful choices in his life. However, his heart for God was never questioned. In 2 Samuel 7, we find the story of David's desire to build God a house of worship. David recognized that while he had a house, God was being worshiped in a tent. This troubled David because it sent the message that the king was more valuable than God. This is what it means to have a heart for God.

In this passage, God made a promise to David: David's rule and kingdom would never end. On the surface, the difficulty with this promise is that the kingdom of Israel did eventually fall. But what God promises often comes about differently than we expect it to. God fully kept this promise because the lineage of David went all the way to Jesus Christ, the true and eternal King of not just Israel but the world. This means that the ultimate kingdom that never ends was brought about through David's lineage. God keeps His promises.

## DELIGHT

**Write down a few things you know about King David. Why do you think God chose to bless David in these specific ways?**

**How is David's heart for God displayed in this passage?**

**When has God kept a promise to you that unfolded in a completely different way than you expected?**

## DISPLAY

Use this time to consider the attitude and condition of your own heart. If someone were to write a story about your life, what words would they use to describe you? Would your life choices show that you had a heart for God? Knowing God's promises from your past, present, and future, think about two things you could do today that would help you to cultivate a heart for God.

**Take a minute or two to practice the following three-step process: 1) Share with God the things that keep you from having a heart for Him. Ask Him for forgiveness. 2) Pray out loud from a passage of God's Word that points you to an obedient heart and mind. 3) Ask God to help you obey. Repeat this process as often as you need to cultivate your heart to follow God.**

## DAY 8

# *He Always Has*

READ ISAIAH 53.

*But he was pierced because of our rebellion,*
*crushed because of our iniquities;*
*punishment for our peace was on him,*
*and we are healed by his wounds.*
*— Isaiah 53:5*

## DISCOVER

Prophets in the Old Testament spoke or wrote what God said. Isaiah wrote down these words from God more than seven hundred years before Jesus's side was pierced on the cross. This prophecy told a story that could only be understood after God's plan for salvation had been revealed.

Have you considered the significance of your "iniquities"? God has laws and ways in which humanity is commanded to live. When you break His law, you are committing iniquity, or sin. On its most base level, sin makes the world unequal. When we commit sin, the punishment we deserve is death.

This is why we need a Messiah; this is why Jesus gave up His life. God's grace and goodness was on display in the life, ministry, death, and resurrection of Jesus Christ. His side was pierced on our behalf. Giving your faith and life to Jesus fully means that you are no longer at war with God; instead, you have peace. Jesus was the punishment that was needed to restore our peace. His death paid our penalty for our sin.

God spoke through the prophet Isaiah to bring hope and encouragement to a people who were struggling. We have the amazing gift that we can read this text today and fully understand what God meant. We see Jesus in every word. You also are able to see God's goodness and faithfulness shown seven hundred years before Jesus arrived. This should bring great hope for your life today. God loves you. He always has.

## DELIGHT

**How do you think humanity is healed by Jesus's wounds? How did Jesus's death "heal" Christians?**

**Read Romans 3:23 and 6:23. How does your sin impact your relationship with God?**

**How does faith in Christ bring forgiveness?**

## DISPLAY

If you can get permission, go grab a vacuum in your house. (If your parents ask too many questions, just tell them it's for Jesus!) Now, take a piece of paper from a notebook and rip it to shreds. Really go for it and make the pieces as small as you can. Take the shreds and toss them all over your bedroom floor. Think about those shreds as a symbol of the iniquities you have committed. Finally, use the vacuum to make every shred disappear. Take a mental picture of what was before and what is after. That's what Jesus has done for you!

**Spend this time thanking God for sending Jesus and for being ever faithful. Thank Him that you are cleaned from sin and shame because of the cross. Finally, ask God to help you remember what He has done and the peace He brings your life.**

DAY 9

# This Changes Everything

READ ISAIAH 61.

*The Spirit of the Lord GOD is on me, because the LORD has anointed me to bring good news to the poor. He has sent me to heal the brokenhearted, to proclaim liberty to the captives and freedom to the prisoners.*
*— Isaiah 61:1*

## DISCOVER

When is the last time you heard good news? Most news comes in the shape of bad things that have happened in the world. Just scrolling through social media or any other news source will let you in on how tough life can be today. During Isaiah's time, the kingdoms of Israel and Judah were falling apart. God's chosen people had chosen to live in selfish and sinful ways, far from God. The consequences of their sin was that the nation of Israel cracked and crumbled and other nations defeated it. The people were spread out all over the earth.

Israel needed good news. Isaiah communicated what God said: God had given him the task of bringing "good news to the poor." Israel was poor. Its people were broken-hearted spiritually, and some physically. When Isaiah wrote this, many were actual prisoners. Today is no different for us. We often choose sin, shame, and selfishness. Our hearts can be poor and brokenhearted. It often feels like we are in spiritual and physical prison.

The best news is the good news of Jesus Christ. God showed us that He loves those who don't deserve it. He cares about the poor, the lonely, and the brokenhearted. Faith in Jesus brings liberty and freedom from the prison of sin. When you give your life to Christ, you are set free. There is no greater news than this.

## DELIGHT

**What does it look like in spiritual terms to be poor, brokenhearted, and a prisoner?**

**In what specific ways does faith in Jesus bring you freedom?**

## DISPLAY

Write about a time when you felt alone and imprisoned by sin or a personal struggle of some sort. You don't have to get too specific in your writing—only write what you are comfortable with. Now, compare that to what it feels like to follow Jesus. Write your understanding of how Jesus sets you free. Draw a line from each struggle to each way Christ sets you free.

**Talk with God about all the ways He has forgiven you and set you free. Ask Him to remind you of what your life was like before Jesus and how you are now different, living in Christ Jesus. Ask God to help you remember that you are free and alive in Christ Jesus. Ask God to help you believe that you are forgiven and free.**

## DAY 10

# *Hope*

READ ISAIAH 40.

*A voice of one crying out: Prepare the way of the Lord in the wilderness; make a straight highway for our God in the desert.*
*— Isaiah 40:3*

## DISCOVER

The first thirty-nine chapters in Isaiah predict the fall of Israel. God promised that Israel would be a great nation, but the people of Israel persisted in chasing after false gods. They chose the most extreme forms of selfishness. Because of their many great sins, Israel was defeated and fell.

Some in Israel felt that God had abandoned them. Isaiah reminded them of God's goodness. Isaiah 40 is a promise that hope was coming. Isaiah said a voice would shout out that the way of the Lord was coming. God would make everything right again, and the whole world would see God's glory.

There are two major details you should understand from these verses. First, God keeps His promises. Prophecy after prophecy in the Old Testament all pointed to Jesus, and each promise was kept. This helps us see the good news for people who trust their lives to God.

Second, God didn't just bring salvation to Israel alone; His glory is for the whole world. If God loved Israel even though its people chose to run from Him, that means that God's love for you is no different. In the middle of whatever spiritual or physical struggle you are facing, God loves you and His love and forgiveness don't change. He keeps His promises.

## DELIGHT

**How have you experienced God's faithfulness in your life?**

**How do these verses bring you hope today?**

**In what way does Jesus make things right for His people?**

## DISPLAY

Choose some blank space anywhere you'd like in this book. In that space, write some words that would describe ways you have chosen to live selfishly and run from God. Write these simple one-word descriptions very lightly in your book. As you write each one, take some time and talk to God about any shame and guilt you have experienced because of those things. After you ask for God's forgiveness, take your pen or pencil and scribble out the word using the shape of a cross. Make this cross over each word as a symbol of what God has done through Jesus. Thank God for His faithfulness in bringing you forgiveness.

**Spend time with God reflecting on all the new ways you've seen Him to be faithful by following His Word. Ask God to show you moments when He has been specifically faithful in your life. Finally, ask God to help you always turn to Him in every part of your life. Ask God to be your only hope.**

## Section 2

# Preparing the Way for the Messiah

**Many awe-inspiring things happened in the days leading up to the coming of the Messiah. In the time between the Old Testament prophecies and the birth of Jesus, there were amazing moments of expectation and hope. When Jesus was born, angels told of his arrival, and humans had to take steps of faith in trusting what God would do. God's promises of the past would be fulfilled in the most spectacular and seemingly impossible ways.**

## DAY 11

# Right Living

READ LUKE 1:5-17.

*"And he will go before him in the spirit and power of Elijah, to turn the hearts of fathers to their children, and the disobedient to the understanding of the righteous, to make ready for the Lord a prepared people." — Luke 1:17*

## DISCOVER

Zechariah was a priest who served in the temple for the Hebrew people. There were thousands of priests who served, and they all had specific jobs. Some priests could live an entire life and never be chosen to enter the temple of the Lord to burn the incense. The fact that Zechariah was chosen to do this was an amazing honor.

Even greater than being chosen for this special job, Zechariah was met by an angel of the Lord while he was doing his priestly duty. The message Zechariah received was shocking: "Your prayer has been answered." What had Zechariah been praying? Priests would typically pray for the salvation of Israel. However, the angel's words brought double blessing.

Zechariah and Elizabeth had not been able to have children. They were past the point physically of being able to have a child and had more than likely stopped asking God for that blessing. This miracle that God did with Zechariah and Elizabeth proved once again that nothing is impossible for God.

Their child would be John the Baptist, the cousin of Jesus. John would be full of the Holy Spirit, and he would be set aside to be the voice crying out in the wilderness, preparing people for the coming of the Lord. It had been four hundred years since a prophet had spoken the words of God. John would go on to preach a message of repentance and preparation. God kept the promise He had made through Isaiah (see Isa. 40).

## DELIGHT

**Has there ever been a point when you were certain God would not answer your prayer, only for Him to do it when you least expected it? What was the prayer? What happened when He answered it?**

**God set John aside for a special purpose: to prepare the way for Jesus. You may not be called to a task like that, but—great or small—what has God called you to do?**

## DISPLAY

Zechariah and Elizabeth were described as "righteous." This was partly because Zechariah had been faithful and obedient to God, even though his life didn't go exactly like he thought it should. He served faithfully in the temple doing what he was supposed to do. Jot down some ways you can be righteous and faithful to God every day in your life and actions.

**Ask God to reveal ways you can be faithful and steady. Ask Him to show you how to make good spiritual habits to help you grow in your trust of Him. Finally, ask God to help you remain faithful to Him, even when your life doesn't go the way you think it should.**

DAY 12

# Nothing: Impossible

READ LUKE 1:18-25.

*"How can I know this?" Zechariah asked the angel. "For I am an old man, and my wife is well along in years."*
*— Luke 1:18*

## DISCOVER

How can it be that a man described as "righteous" didn't believe the message an angel gave him inside the temple of the Lord? The answer is very easy: Zechariah was human. Even righteous people struggle to trust God with everything. Gabriel's message was clear, but Zechariah was filled with doubts. So, the angel gave the priest a constant reminder of the truth of God's Word by taking Zechariah's words away.

Zechariah had used his mouth to preach God's Word his whole life. It must have been unimaginable to no longer be able to speak. It caused such a scene when he came out of the temple that everyone must have known Zechariah experienced something powerful from the Lord.

One of the beautiful things God often does when making a promise is to give a confirmation of the promise in some way. It was one thing for Zechariah to hear with his own ears that God would allow Elizabeth to get pregnant. But when he saw his spouse showing physical signs of this pregnancy, that was confirmation of God's promise before his very eyes. As Zechariah watched the baby grow, can you imagine the joy he felt and the assurance he could visibly see of God's provision and love?

Elizabeth's story concludes this text by describing the disgrace she felt from not being able to have a child. Let this be a reminder that God gives grace to His people. He loves, He blesses, and He gives grace.

## DELIGHT

**What were the reasons Zechariah shared for not being able to believe the angel?**

**Is there another story we're read from the Old Testament that reminds you of this story? How are the passages similar? How are they different?**

## DISPLAY

What are some things you struggle to believe? Although you've more than likely never spoken with the angel Gabriel, there are definitely some miraculous things you have experienced. If you've given your life to Christ, you've been empowered with the Holy Spirit—the presence of God in your life. He helps you to have the fruit of the Spirit (see Gal. 5:22-23). He also helps you to know what God calls you to do. The Word of God is confirmed by the Holy Spirit. But do you believe that God has forgiven you? Do you believe that God loves you unconditionally? Do you believe God's Word when it says that you are a new creation in Christ Jesus?

**Today's prayer is very simple: Pray that God will give you faith like Elizabeth displayed.**

## DAY 13

# Deliverer

READ LUKE 1:26-33.

*Then the angel told her, "Do not be afraid, Mary, for you have found favor with God. Now listen: You will conceive and give birth to a son, and you will name him Jesus."*
*— Luke 1:30-31*

## DISCOVER

Mary was most likely between thirteen and sixteen years old at the time of this angelic visitation. It seems perfectly understandable for a teenager to be troubled by an angel showing up and calling her "favored" by God. When God reveals Himself to people, there should always be a sense of awe and wonder.

Mary was a faithful young woman who knew the words and promises of God. The angel explained something to her that left no room for doubt. The name Jesus means "deliverer." When the angel said that Jesus would be "great," that means something more significant than we are used to. After all, we say everything is "great": pizza, television shows, our favorite teachers. But in Hebrew culture, *great* was a far more impactful word. "Son of the Most High" can be understood no other way. When you put it all together, here's what it added up to: Mary was going to have a baby, and that baby was going to be the Messiah who God had promised the people of Israel. Mary's child was going to be the King of the kingdom that has no end.

To this day, God continues to share His Word. He does not lie, mislead, or confuse. When God promises something, it will come to be. God promised a Messiah, and Mary was the first to know that Messiah's name would be Jesus.

## DELIGHT

**What are some of the promises God made to Mary through Gabriel?**

**How does God deliver you today?**

## DISPLAY

Mary's expectation of life and what others knew about her changed dramatically when she met with an angel of the Lord. She went from being a faithful young woman to knowing she was favored by God. How have you changed since Jesus entered your life? How has Jesus delivered you from sin and darkness?

**Ask God to remind you of all the ways He loves you and has forgiven you in Christ Jesus.**

## DAY 14

# Servant Heart

READ LUKE 1:34-38.

*"See, I am the Lord's servant," said Mary.*
*"May it happen to me as you have said." Then the angel left her.*
*— Luke 1:38*

## DISCOVER

Yesterday you read the passage right before Mary's response. She essentially heard that she would become pregnant and her child would be named Jesus, the promised Messiah of the world. Consider what it would be like to be Mary at that moment. There would probably be lots of questions running through your mind. The one question recorded in Scripture from this event was extremely practical. Mary was not married. She had been faithful to God in her actions before marriage and was still a virgin. How could she be pregnant? As far as she could see, what the angel had told her was impossible.

Gabriel's response explained the impossible. The presence of God would overshadow her and God would place a baby in her womb. God confirmed He was doing the impossible in another way, too: not only did He place a baby in a virgin, but He also blessed Mary's relative Elizabeth with pregnancy, even though she was old and had not been able to have a child before. Nothing is impossible for God.

Mary and Elizabeth's pregnancies are beautiful reminders of God's faithfulness in the present and hope for the future. Jesus changed Mary's entire life. She would go on to see Jesus's life and ministry. She would watch as her son was wrongly convicted and put to death. She also experienced the joy of His resurrection. She served God well. But it all began when she was faithful to God as a teenager.

## DELIGHT

**What do you think it means to serve the Lord?**

**What are some ways Mary acted faithfully in the middle of an extremely unique situation?**

**What types of things has God called you to do, even though you didn't know what the outcome would be?**

## DISPLAY

Think about some of your favorite Bible verses. Do any of those verses offer promises from God? If so, think about what it means to believe God even when you don't know what the outcome will be. Mary's example of trusting God in the middle of uncertainty is a wonderful picture of how we are called to live. Write down a few of those special verses through which you have felt God speak to you, and think about how you can trust God as Mary did.

**As you are praying, share these verse with God out loud. Tell Him what they mean to you. Ask God to give you strength and courage to have faith like Mary.**

## DAY 15

# Compassion

READ MATTHEW 1:18-21.

*"She will give birth to a son, and you are to name him Jesus, because he will save his people from their sins."*
*— Matthew 1:21*

## DISCOVER

I struggle to imagine what Joseph must have felt like. He was engaged to Mary. As was the custom in their day, their parents had talked and agreed that it was a good match. Mary was supposedly virtuous. His future was set. He probably dreamed what it would be like to lead his own household and have children who would follow in his footsteps as carpenters. Then he discovered that Mary was pregnant.

By Hebrew law, two options were available to Joseph. Although they were not technically husband and wife yet, they were betrothed, which by law was as good as married. He could either have her put to death for her sin, or he could choose to divorce her quietly by signing a piece of paper in the presence of two witnesses. Joseph decided not to put her to shame. Perhaps he figured that her parents could find a new match for her to marry before her belly showed too much. Then Mary could move on with her life. He made a choice of compassion and love for someone who, as far as he knew, didn't deserve it.

Joseph was a person of faith who acted rightly. At this time in Joseph's life, he didn't know what his future held. It probably felt like his present was falling apart. But even in the middle of his pain, he showed compassion.

## DELIGHT

**Joseph chose compassion in the middle of what was potentially the most difficult moment of his life. How can you choose to be compassionate to others even when you are going through struggles?**

**Why does living justly not equal to an easy life?**

## DISPLAY

Jot down a few times you've felt like you were doing the right thing and got mistreated for it. Think about how you felt and what you did in response. Was it kind, just, or right? Did you show compassion to others or did you attempt to pay them back for what happened to you?

Consider the cross. Jesus did nothing wrong and did not deserve the treatment He was given. Yet in His love for us, God gave up His Son so that we could have our sins covered. We were made right before God and gained access to eternal life through our faith. If Jesus was treated unjustly for you, how must you respond to others when you are mistreated?

**Ask God to help you act in kindness, mercy, and compassion, even in difficult times.**

## DAY 16

# God with Us

READ MATTHEW 1:22-25.

*"See, the virgin will become pregnant and give birth to a son, and they will name him Immanuel, which is translated 'God is with us'."*
*— Matthew 1:23*

## DISCOVER

Joseph had been raised knowing that he belonged to the house and lineage of David. Since the time of David's reign, there had been prophecy that the Messiah would come through his descendants (see 2 Sam 7:16). Joseph heard this at the temple. He probably heard it at home. At every special Jewish holiday, there was talk of a Messiah. This concept was ingrained in his daily life.

During the most difficult time in his life to that point, Joseph was considering what his next steps were. He was thinking about how to quietly divorce Mary, only to experience a vision from an angel. The words that the angel spoke to him were probably familiar: the angel was quoting from the book of Isaiah (see Isa. 7:14). But to hear it in this context, knowing that his wife-to-be was the virgin in question? The Messiah was coming to save the world from their sins. It was Joseph's family, the house of David, to which Jesus would be born. Everything he had ever heard and been taught was coming true, and it wasn't just happening in his time—it was happening to him personally.

Joseph woke up from his sleep and went to Mary. He agreed to marry her, but they didn't consummate their marriage until after the baby was born. The son of God was born just as God had promised. This story is one of every day people practicing faith and trust in God. It is also a story of a God who loves His people and keeps His promises.

## DELIGHT

**How does the name "Immanuel" also explain what God did in the lives of Mary and Joseph?**

**In what specific ways did Joseph and Mary listen to God and practice obedience? How can you follow their example today?**

## DISPLAY

Think, say, and do. These are three things that we see Mary and Joseph practice in their lives. How can you practice faith in your life? Think through the following questions:

- How does what you think impact what you say?
- How does what you say impact how you live?
- How have you hidden God's Word in your heart and mind?
- Do you think about what God wants you to think about?
- Do you fill your mind with pure and good things?
- How does your speech reflect your mind?
- How do your words show people love, grace, kindness, gentleness, and mercy?
- Do you keep your word? That is, do you actually do what you say you are going to do?

Think, say, and do. It's all connected.

**Ask God to help you to take steps of faith in your thoughts, your words, and your actions.**

## Memory Verse

◆

**See, the virgin will become pregnant and give birth to a son, and they will name him Immanuel, which is translated "God is with us."**

◆

*Matthew 1:23*

**DAY 17**

# Leaping Baby

READ LUKE 1:39-45.

*When Elizabeth heard Mary's greeting, the baby leaped inside her, and Elizabeth was filled with the Holy Spirit.*
*— Luke 1:41*

## DISCOVER

An angel had visited Mary, and Joseph had been given a vision. There were only a few other people on earth who might believe what they had just experienced. So Mary had to go see someone who would understand the amazing things that were happening to her. Elizabeth would understand; amazing things were happening to her, too.

Just as an angel had visited Joseph, an angel had visited Elizabeth's husband, Zechariah, about their son. One of the things the angel told Zechariah was that their son would be filled with the Holy Spirit. The presence of God would surround him and guide his steps. We know later that their son, John, would be the one to let everyone know exactly who Jesus was. Yet, in that moment, even before these two men were born, John leapt for joy in his mother's womb when Mary came near Elizabeth.

Immediately, Elizabeth was filled with the Spirit and praised God at the arrival of the mother of her Lord. What a beautiful moment Scripture captures for us. Why did Elizabeth celebrate? Why did both Mary and Elizabeth experience such joy? Because God used this moment to confirm everything He had said to them. They had heard and believed, but now they saw with their own eyes. The salvation of humanity was coming to the world through this baby being formed in Mary's womb.

## DELIGHT

**Mary and Elizabeth could each relate to what the other was going through. Who are the people who understand you and what you're going though and who encourage you to be like Jesus?**

**How do you think this moment could have helped both women prepare for the rest of their pregnancies and their lives as parents of such special children?**

## DISPLAY

Reflect on a time when someone showed up in your life at the right time to remind you of God's goodness, faithfulness, or mercy. Think about how you needed God to confirm something in your life and He used this person to do that. Write out a few words that describe what the situation was like before this person showed up and how things changed after their words of wisdom. Consider a few other ways God has helped you to make it through situations because of other Christians in your faith community. Finally, write down a few ways you could listen to God's Spirit calling you to do the same for other people.

**Ask God to show you a few ways He has used others to provide encouragement to you and to help you see His plan for your life. Pray that God will help you to listen when He calls you to do the same for other people. Thank God for His great care and love for you.**

## DAY 18

# *Stay Humble*

READ LUKE 1:46-56.

*And Mary said: My soul magnifies the Lord,*
*and my spirit rejoices in God my Savior.*
*— Luke 1:46-47*

## DISCOVER

What do you think it would have been like to be in Mary's shoes? It might have been easy to get a big head. Mary was chosen by God to deliver not just any baby but the Christ child into the world! However, Mary's response was not to get a swollen ego. We know her heart because we can read her song.

Mary's takeaway from her experience was the goodness of God. Rather than focus on herself and her own special situation, she saw God's mighty goodness. She pointed out how holy God was for what He was doing to save generation after generation. She pointed out that God had taken a nobody and made her a somebody. The only thing Mary wanted to do was worship and rejoice in the God who saves. Thoughts, heart, soul, and actions, she wanted to celebrate the greatness of God for bringing the Messiah into the world. Mary understood the significance of what was happening. God would keep His promise, and the world would be saved through Israel. Everything God had promised Abraham would be fulfilled.

Mary understood that God's choice was to bring salvation to the world through humble circumstances. Rather than sending His Savior in on a white horse to destroy the enemies of Israel, God sent Him as a baby. And rather than choosing a queen or important figure to bear this baby, it would be a young woman whose most important possession was her faith. God would use humble people to bring His mighty, saving love to the world.

## DELIGHT

**Describe a few ways Mary reacted to what God had done. What are some ways Mary described God?**

**How does Mary's song reveal God's plan since the beginning?**

## DISPLAY

Have you ever written a song? In the space below take a moment and write your own poem or song about God's story in your life. You don't have to be fancy about it. Use Mary's example as a guide. Write about what God has done for you, who God is, and how God's plan—fulfilled through Jesus—saved you.

**Find a private place where you can sing the song you wrote above out loud as a prayer to God. Remember, no one will hear it but God. Don't worry about your pitch or tone; just use this moment as a time to celebrate what God has done for you. Take your song and make it a song of praise to God.**

## DAY 19

# God's Plan for Your Life

READ LUKE 1:57-66.

*All who heard about him took it to heart, saying, "What then will this child become?" For, indeed, the Lord's hand was with him.*
*— Luke 1:66*

## DISCOVER

Naming a child is an important task. Some people want to make sure their child will have a name that won't sound like anyone else's. Others choose a name that will help that child carry on a rich family history. Zechariah and Elizabeth thought that their ability to have children had long passed them by, yet God had done the impossible. They saw no higher honor than to name this son after his father. But God had specific plans for John.

What joy Zechariah must have felt as he watched Elizabeth's belly grow. But remember, Zechariah couldn't speak: God had taken away his voice. No one heard a word from him the entire time Elizabeth was pregnant. In these verses, Elizabeth said they would break from the tradition of naming a child after family members or the father. Instead, their child would be called John. When they turned to the mute Zechariah, he found a way to let everyone know this was what God wanted. As soon as it was decided, Zechariah was able to speak.

From the time John was conceived, he brought joy and wonder to everyone around him. The news spread throughout the region: God was up to something. It was evident that John would make an impact on the world. He would declare the coming of the Lord.

## DELIGHT

**Why do you think the Bible says that people recognized God's mercy toward Elizabeth because of John's birth?**

**How does Zechariah speaking again after nine months of silence point to God doing something miraculous?**

## DISPLAY

While you probably weren't born after a prediction from an angel, your life is special. You belong to God, and He has created you for His glory. Spend a few moments considering the purpose for which God has created you. You might not be a pastor or a career missionary in the far unreached places in the world, but no matter your life's calling, you can be a person who uses your gifts for God's kingdom. Write down some of the specific qualities or gifts with which God has blessed you and how you might use them—not just in the future, but right now. If you're stuck, think about other people you know whom you admire. Think about how you might do what you've seen them do.

**Ask God to give you clear direction for how you can use your unique gifts and talents in such a way that He will receive the glory, not you.**

**DAY 20**

# *Heart Prep*

READ LUKE 1:67-80.

*Because of our God's merciful compassion, the dawn from on high will visit us to shine on those who live in darkness and the shadow of death, to guide our feet into the way of peace.*
*— Luke 1:78-79*

## DISCOVER

Zechariah finally spoke! After nine months of waiting for this opportunity, the Spirit of God filled up his mind with words to be heard. A few specific themes came to the forefront in Zechariah's prophecy. He began by praising and worshiping God for who He is and what He had done. Words and phrases like *blessed, salvation, raised up, deliverer*, and *forgiveness* flowed from Zechariah's mouth.

He also pointed out how all of God's words and promises were connected. He mentioned the promises that God had made to both Abraham and David, over a thousand years apart from each other. He reminded the people of the covenant promise that God made with Israel and how God kept His promises. Finally, he prophesied about his son John and the role he would have in ushering in the Messiah.

Jesus is the Most High, and John is the prophet who told everyone of His coming. John's message was one of repentance and preparation for the Messiah's arrival. He carried out the vow of a Nazarite and lived his days away from the world, preparing for his message of repentance to be heard. John was the "voice crying out from the wilderness."

## DELIGHT

**After nine months of silence, Zechariah finally was able to speak again, and he had a lot to say. When has God's Word and goodness welled up this vividly in your life?**

**Zechariah said that Jesus's arrival was due to God's "merciful compassion." How have you experienced God's merciful compassion in your life?**

## DISPLAY

Zechariah had nine months to consider all the things God had said about both his future son and the Messiah. Then the Holy Spirit filled him and he spoke truth that brought hope to God's people. What do you hope for? Take some time today and prayerfully consider your future. Think about what God might be calling you to do or how He might be calling you to live. Write down some of your hopes and dreams about what could come next for you. Do those ideas line up with the gospel and faithful Christian living?

**Ask God to help you see His truth from Scripture as a guide to obedient steps of faith for your future. Ask God to help you dream about what He might be calling you to do.**

## Section 3

# The Birth of the Messiah

**Jesus showed up for everyone. In this section, you'll see that God revealed His Savior to both the lowest of the low and the most famous in the land. From shepherds to kings, everyone wanted to know more about Jesus when He was born in Bethlehem. This should bring great encouragement to you. If God cares about everyone, that means He certainly cares about you.**

## DAY 21

# *What's a Manger?*

READ LUKE 2:1-7.

*Then she gave birth to her firstborn son, and she wrapped him tightly in cloth and laid him in a manger, because there was no guest room available for them.*
*— Luke 2:7*

## DISCOVER

The very first sentence in Luke 2 highlights the immense power of Caesar Augustus. He made a law that the "whole world"—that is, the entire Roman empire—should be taxed. Because of this decree, people under his rule from everywhere had to go back to their ancestral hometowns, no matter where they lived.

To comply with this decree, Mary and Joseph had to travel eighty miles back to the home of Joseph's ancestors—Bethlehem. No one made a big fuss that they were going there. There was no royal parade for the soon-to-be-born King or His parents. This is peak humility on display. If we look at Caesar and Jesus side by side, the contrast is stark.

Christ's birth has been so celebrated that we can't think of anything but Christmas festivities and nativity scenes when we hear the word "manger." But the manger Jesus laid in was far from the peaceful bed we imagine today. There were animals that had been doing animal things everywhere. No amount of fresh hay would sanitize that situation. Jesus was born in the most humble of circumstances.

The ultimate version of humility came in the form of the Messiah being born as a helpless baby. Jesus was the opposite of power and authority. The God of the universe humbled Himself to the point of taking on human form and dwelling among us. This was God's plan for salvation: a humble, fragile human who understood everything humanity went through, yet never sinned.

## DELIGHT

**List all the examples of humility you see in this passage. How do God's examples of humility point you towards a life of service?**

**What can these verses teach us about the difference between the power of a man (Caesar Augustus) versus God's plan?**

## DISPLAY

Make a plan today to practice humility. Think about how you could spend a full day putting others before yourself. Today is the perfect time to think of all the ways Jesus put others before Himself all the way to the cross. Plan your day, but don't tell anyone about your plans. After your "humble" day, take some notes on how you felt and how you made others feel. Compare this to what Jesus calls us to do.

**Talk to God about living a life of service to others because of what Christ has done for you. Ask God to help you grow in humility for His glory.**

DAY 22

# *Even Shepherds*

READ LUKE 2:8-14.

*But the angel said to them, "Don't be afraid, for look, I proclaim to you good news of great joy that will be for all the people: Today in the city of David a Savior was born for you, who is the Messiah, the Lord."*
*— Luke 2:10-11*

## DISCOVER

Shepherds in the time of Jesus weren't popular people. God had created a system for people to be forgiven of their sins by sacrificing unblemished animals, and following this system was mandatory for the people of Israel. Sheep were necessary for worship. Still, the shepherds who cared for those sheep were seen as unclean because they had to work with these filthy animals for their living. Shepherds were considered very lowly in the eyes of Hebrew people.

Shepherds lived on the edge of town, and the type of people who filled this role were often those who couldn't do more prestigious jobs. It was a necessary job that no one wanted to do. Yet God chose to reveal His plan for salvation to shepherds in the most fantastic of ways. On the edge of town, to an unlikely group of people, the birth of the Messiah was announced by a choir of angels!

When God does things, it's for a reason. Look at these points of connection. David was a shepherd; Jesus was a descendant of David. David was considered a man after God's own heart; shepherds have a heart for sheep. Many times in Scripture God's people are called sheep; Jesus is the Good Shepherd. The blood of an unblemished lamb was sprinkled on the altar to cover the sins of the people; Jesus was the perfect sacrifice for our sins. When God declared that a Savior was born, He wanted the world to know that the Savior was for all people—even shepherds.

## DELIGHT

**Why do you think the shepherds were filled with great fear? How would you have responded?**

**In your life, who are the people who are looked down upon and not respected? How can you show them the same love that God showed the shepherds?**

## DISPLAY

Even though the shepherds might have known some things about God, on that night they learned about God firsthand when He spoke to them. How might this have changed their lives forever? In the space below, write down a few key points of your spiritual story. Write about the first moment you remember having a spiritual conversation with God. Tell about the moment you decided to give your life to Jesus. Finally, jot down what God is doing today in your life because of your salvation. Read over all of this to remember all the ways that God has worked in your life.

**Thank God for revealing Himself to you. Ask Him to help you live differently because of Jesus Christ and your salvation through Him. Ask God to give you courage to share what you know about Jesus with other people.**

## DAY 23

# *Tell What You've Seen*

READ LUKE 2:15-20.

*The shepherds returned, glorifying and praising God for all the things they had seen and heard, which were just as they had been told.*
*— Luke 2:20*

## DISCOVER

Sometimes when we read stories in Scripture, the real excitement of the moment doesn't quite translate. "Let's go straight to Bethlehem" sounds kind of low key. "They hurried off" helps a little. Use your Spirit-led imagination right now to imagine what it might have been like for the shepherds that night. What would you have done in their shoes? Maybe you would have screamed, or shouted, or even shaken with excitement at the thought of finding the Messiah in a manger.

What do you think it was like when they found baby Jesus and His parents? Joseph must have been concerned. He had taken his pregnant wife on an eighty mile journey, and when they arrived, they had been provided with nothing more than a rough, animal-filled barn. Now the Messiah was laying in an animal trough while a bunch of stinky shepherds were losing their minds in worship. You can't help but laugh and be in awe at the thought of this moment.

Topping all of this off, the shepherds shared word-for-word what God had told them and why they were there. Can you imagine how this must have felt to Mary and Joseph? Scripture says that Mary gathered up every memory as a treasure in her heart.

Finally, these same shepherds didn't go home quietly: they went home praising and glorifying God. It's a wonder anyone in that small town slept at all that night. Little did they know that God had come near.

## DELIGHT

**What is the value of treasuring something in your heart? What are the things that you treasure?**

**As you imagine yourself living out the experience of the shepherds, what do you think your response would have been?**

## DISPLAY

Yesterday you spent time thinking about your testimony—how God revealed Himself to you and how you responded. Today, take a moment to consider how you can effectively tell people about what you have experienced. Do you know what you would say word-for-word to someone? Using the space below or a separate piece of paper, write one paragraph that could be used for your testimony. Remember, we've been talking about humility, so be careful to spend time talking about God's greatness, mercy, and forgiveness that came to you because of Jesus.

Practice sharing your testimony out loud to yourself in a mirror, or even record it on your phone. Think about how you might make it more clear. After you have got it down, start praying about how you could share it with others.

**Ask God today to help you have an opportunity to share the story of what Jesus has done in your life with someone who needs to hear it.**

## DAY 24

# Church

READ LUKE 2:21-24.

*And when the days of their purification according to the law of Moses were finished, they brought him up to Jerusalem to present him to the Lord.*
*— Luke 2:22*

## DISCOVER

It's not easy going to church. You've had a long week with lots of homework and maybe practice of some kind before or after school. Plus you've got to make sure you're doing all the things your parents are asking you to do at home. Then you still want to make time to watch videos on the internet, play video games, or hang out with your friends. Trying to fit church attendance into our weekly lives can be difficult when you measure all the other things we have to—and want to—do. So, why do we do it? Keep reading.

Mary and Joseph spent time feeding and changing diapers for the Savior of the world. What's the point of going to church when you have God Himself with you? Yet Mary and Joseph still chose to take their child to the temple on the eighth day as the law of Moses told them to do. What was the point? Mary and Joseph understood the significance of being faithful to what God had called them to do in faith community.

The temple was the place where Israelites met and worshiped God. Today, faithful church attendance is the way we are reminded on a weekly basis about how we are called to live for God in our daily life. We get to encourage other Christians to be faithful in their lives, and they encourage us to do the same. We get to sing together of the goodness of God. We observe baptism and the Lord's Supper. These things don't save us, but they do strengthen us in our faith. Mary and Joseph understood the importance of worshiping God in community as He called them to. We should too.

## DELIGHT

**What was the value of presenting Jesus to the Lord? Why would Mary and Joseph do this since they knew that Jesus *is* the Lord?**

**What do you think Mary and Joseph's obedience taught Jesus? Why is this important?**

## DISPLAY

Take some time to consider your church involvement. If you are already involved in a faith community, take time to write down some of the substantial benefits you've seen for your faith life, as well as ways you've been able to serve others. Then, use the concordance or index in the back of your Bible or search the internet to find some things that the Bible says about being part of a church and why it's significant. Write a few of these verses down. If you don't attend church regularly, take some time to ask yourself why you might consider it. What things are keeping you from making that commitment?

**Ask God to bring other Christians into your life to help you live faithfully for Jesus. Thank God for your church, and ask Him how you can serve others for His glory.**

**DAY 25**

# A Pierced Heart

READ LUKE 2:25-35.

*Then Simeon blessed them and told his mother Mary, "Indeed, this child is destined to cause the fall and rise of many in Israel and to be a sign that will be opposed — and a sword will pierce your own soul — that the thoughts of many hearts may be revealed."*
*— Luke 2:34-35*

## DISCOVER

Raising Jesus was far from normal. In His first few weeks of life, God sent a few important people to help Mary and Joseph get a glimpse into their future, including Simeon. We don't know a lot about him other than a few interesting facts: he was righteous, he was committed to God, and he longed for Israel to see salvation. He was so faithful in his relationship with God that God granted Simeon the knowledge that the Messiah would arrive in his lifetime. Simeon had been waiting and watching.

One day, Simeon was led by the Spirit to the temple. He saw Mary and Joseph, and then he saw the child. Simeon walked up and held Jesus, then he proclaimed some important words. Simeon shared with the parents that Jesus was the "prince of peace" promised by Isaiah (see Isa. 9:6-7). Jesus would bring salvation to not only Israel but the whole world.

The moment must have been magical . . . until Simeon shared one last thing with Mary: the words "a sword will pierce your own soul" (Luke 2:35). What did Mary think in this moment? We don't know, but we do know what Mary would experience in her life. She would see Jesus suffer. She would see a sword pierce His side. She would watch as Jesus's own people rejected Him. At the same time, she would bear witness to what God did in the life, death, and resurrection of her son. Mary's faith helped her to trust God through every step she experienced.

## DELIGHT

**How did Simeon's message confirm what Joseph and Mary already knew?**

**How did Simeon's message prepare Mary for future heartache?**

## DISPLAY

In most cases, it isn't possible for us to see God's direct plan until after it has happened. Then we can often see how God was equipping and preparing us along the way. Take some time in the space below and write out a few tough or difficult moments you have had. How did God prepare you beforehand to be able to make it through these tough times? Describe how God's provision, protection, and love helped you make it through those challenges.

**Spend time today thanking God for all the ways He shaped you in the past to help you in your present and your future. Ask God to help you grow in trust and faith when it comes to your future. Thank Him for being present and with you, no matter what you face.**

DAY 26

# Don't Give Up Hope

READ LUKE 2:36-40.

*At that very moment, she came up and began to thank God and to speak about him to all who were looking forward to the redemption of Jerusalem.*
*— Luke 2:38*

## DISCOVER

For many hundreds of years, the people of Israel had come to meet God at the temple. There is no mistake that when Jesus arrived at the temple as a baby, signs and wonders were happening. Simeon gave his special blessing, then Anna did the same. Both were devout and both received words from God. One of the things that separated Anna and Simeon from many others was their belief in a Messiah who would arrive as God had promised.

It had been four hundred years since a prophet from God spoke to Israel. Things had been quiet for so long that people began to believe that God had abandoned them. The hope for a savior had dwindled. Yet this was God's plan and timing all along.

Anna had devoted her life to God so much that she no longer left the temple. Her prayers led her to fast, showing her total reliance on God. Anna never gave up hope that God would keep His promises. She had been old enough to be married for ninety-one years and had lived alone for eighty-four of them. But not only did she never give up, she got to see Jesus with her own eyes.

## DELIGHT

**How old would you guess Anna was? Why do you think she continued to stick around the temple the way she did?**

**People had seen Anna in the temple every day for many years. When she began to talk about the redemption of Israel, what do you imagine these people thought?**

## DISPLAY

Faithfulness and hope: these are two things we see in Anna's life. In the space below, take some time to consider how much you have practiced faith and hope. Do you believe the promises God makes about salvation and being made new in Christ Jesus? How do your actions model a steady life of faith? How can you be more hopeful in your situation right now? What can you do that Anna and Simeon also did?

**Spend some time in your prayers today talking with God about how you can increase your faith and hope. Look to the biblical examples of Anna and Simeon and talk with God about prayer, fasting, and being led by the Spirit. Ask God what that would look like for you today.**

## *Memory Verse*

**But the angel said to them, "Don't be afraid, for look, I proclaim to you good news of great joy that will be for all the people: Today in the city of David a Savior was born for you, who is the Messiah, the Lord."**

*Luke 2:10-11*

**DAY 27**

# Control

READ MATTHEW 2:1-6.

*"And you, Bethlehem, in the land of Judah, are by no means least among the rulers of Judah: Because out of you will come a ruler who will shepherd my people Israel."*
*— Matthew 2:6*

## DISCOVER

Have you ever wondered where the wise men came from? This is a marvelous example of God's faithfulness throughout time. Israel had disobeyed God so extremely that God eventually allowed the kingdom to fall. The people were spread and scattered all over the world. One of those people was a young man named Daniel, who was placed in leadership in Babylon.

Daniel remained faithful to God, and because of this faith, Daniel was put in charge of all the magicians in Babylon. What do you think Daniel taught those magicians? He passed his faith on to them! Hundreds of years later, those magi watched the stars and traveled from a far away land to see this prediction of the Messiah come true.

Some of Herod's smartest and brightest could have also told him the town the Christ would be born in based on prophecy. But as we learned yesterday, many had given up hope and were no longer paying attention. Micah 5:2 prophesied that He would be born in Bethlehem. The wise men were headed that way also. As Herod read the signs, he realized he might have an rival to his throne being born right under his nose. Herod wanted to use this sign as an opportunity to increase his power. God was able to take this moment and use it for His glory by only further confirming for Mary and Joseph that He would protect and provide. The gifts the wise men brought probably made it financially possible for them to flee Herod's evil plan when the time was right.

## DELIGHT

**Based on verse 2, why do you think the arrival of the wise men made Herod nervous?**

**Herod is a prime example of how people can respond to God negatively. Why do you think Herod was more interested in killing Jesus than worshiping Him?**

## DISPLAY

Throughout this book, you have been tasked with reflecting on God's control and authority throughout time. Spend a moment today thinking about what that means for your life. If prayer is essentially submitting to God everything in your heart, then in the form of a written prayer, put down everything in your life that you are afraid of in the present or future. Next to each concern, write down a similar situation you've read about in this book and how it points to God's goodness, authority, and control.

**Ask God to help you trust Him with every concern or worry you have about the present and future. Ask God to help you trust His control. Tell God that you want His will and His way in your life.**

## DAY 28

# God is Wiser

READ MATTHEW 2:7-12.

*Entering the house, they saw the child with Mary his mother, and falling to their knees, they worshiped him. Then they opened their treasures and presented him with gifts: gold, frankincense, and myrrh.*
*— Matthew 2:11*

## DISCOVER

The wise men were almost the exact opposite of shepherds. They had a chest of riches they traveled with just to give away. They could get an audience with King Herod upon their arrival. The shepherds, on the other hand, couldn't get close to town unless it was to bring their sheep to be sacrificed at the temple. Jesus was for shepherds as well as for kings.

Upon seeing Jesus, the wise men presented Mary and Joseph with three gifts, the type of gifts that were only given to a king. It's possible Mary and Joseph were more uncomfortable with the wise men showing up than they were the shepherds! However, at this point in the life of Jesus, so much had already happened that Joseph and Mary were probably just fine with noble, wealthy people showing up.

The events that led to the wise men appearing only further confirm that not only is Jesus for everyone and anyone who believes, but also that God was in control and in charge of all things. No one was or is more powerful.

## DELIGHT

**God is for the richest of the rich, the poorest of the poor, and everyone in between. What needs to happen in your life for you to believe this?**

**How did God tell the wise men to not return to Herod? How does this further confirm God's power?**

## DISPLAY

If Jesus came for everyone, what does that mean for you, your friends, your family, and your community? Think about the implications: Jesus didn't just show up for people who thought they already had everything figured out. Jesus came for sinners. He came for messed up people. God's love was for both the lowly and the majestic, as well as everyone in between. How can you better understand God's love through His love for others? Take a moment to make a list of people you know, then carefully consider their spiritual journey. Think about how you could share with them that Jesus is for them.

**Pray that the Holy Spirit would open up opportunities for you to share the gospel will all kinds of people. Pray that God would give you the courage to speak boldly.**

**DAY 29**

# God's Power is Greater

READ MATTHEW 2:13-15.

*He stayed there until Herod's death, so that what was spoken by the Lord through the prophet might be fulfilled: Out of Egypt I called my Son.*
*— Matthew 2:15*

## DISCOVER

Has your family ever gone on a trip out of state or out of the country? Did you ever consider how much something like that costs? Mary and Joseph were faced with an alarming decision. Joseph had been given yet another dream telling him that they needed to run to Egypt to protect Jesus from Herod. Herod was planning to take out this young child before Jesus could come and take Herod's power. How could Joseph, a humble carpenter, pay for his family to take such a trip like this? It's a good thing wise men visited and dropped off kingly gifts!

This is also a strong reminder that the enemies of God weren't interested in seeing Jesus come to power. They may not have fully understood what this Christ child would do, but it threatened their control of what small power they had. It also highlights the foolish thinking of humanity. God's plans can't be thwarted by human rulers. God used wise men to provide poor people the means to run from an evil king intent on destroying Jesus. All of this is further proof that God is in control of all things.

There are dark forces in this world that are interested in attempting to stop God's will and His way. While God is all powerful, we shouldn't be lulled into thinking that evil won't come and try to make us stumble from time to time. The good news is that God has overcome evil through the life, death, and resurrection of Jesus.

## DELIGHT

**Why do you think people were out to harm Jesus, even when He was a baby?**

**How does this passage further display God's power?**

## DISPLAY

There are many forms of evil in this world. There is the selfish nature we all have that compels us to live our lives the ways we think are best instead of following God. There is also the darkness of the fallen world we live in, where selfishness has ruined the broader world as a whole. Then there is the broken nature of sin throughout the world that causes suffering, shame, sickness, war, and disease. Finally there are the forces of Satan. Spend some time reflecting on how God's power is on display through the promises He has kept and through His act of bringing Jesus to earth. How does this give you hope for today?

**For sixty seconds, just sit silently before God. Then, ask Him to help you listen to Him, just as Joseph listened to Him. Sit in silence for sixty more seconds. If God spoke to you, obey. If you need to sit in silence longer, stay still. Open your heart to whatever He wants to do in you and however He wants to lead you.**

**DAY 30**

# The Details

READ MATTHEW 2:16-23.

*After Herod died, an angel of the Lord appeared in a dream to Joseph in Egypt, saying, "Get up, take the child and his mother, and go to the land of Israel, because those who intended to kill the child are dead."*
*— Matthew 2:19-20*

## DISCOVER

So much happened in the young life of Jesus. Joseph and Mary really went through some trying times. They stayed in Bethlehem after Jesus was born only to run away to Egypt. While it wasn't for many years, they still left everything they knew to keep Him safe.

Upon hearing that Herod had died, they were directed by God to head back home. But when they got home they realized that Herod's son was in power and was just as corrupt as his father was. Joseph didn't feel safe returning to Judea. So, they headed to Galilee and settled down in Nazareth. This seemed like a good place to hopefully live in peace.

Another way that God is truly amazing: seven hundred years earlier, the prophet Isaiah had predicted this very thing would happen (see Isa.11:1). This is yet another example of how powerful and mighty God is: He can use our fears and concerns for His glory. God took care of Joseph, Mary, and Jesus, and He would continue to show His power through the details of Jesus's life.

## DELIGHT

**How has God taken care of the details in your life?**

**Does God care about only the big things or the little things in your life? How do you know?**

## DISPLAY

God takes care of you. Spend some time writing down a few ways God has shown His care in your past and your present. How might He show His care in your future and into eternity? There is no greater example of God's care than the way He sent His Son, Jesus, to come near and live on earth. Jesus paid the ultimate penalty for our sins and did not deserve it. This is God caring for you. In Christ Jesus you can be forgiven and made whole. God cares for you in this way, but He also wants you to turn to Him with your daily needs. God wants you to talk to Him about everything you need.

**Ask God to help you to turn to Him with every single need, concern, and care you have. Ask Him to help you trust that He will provide. Thank Him for the saving work of Jesus Christ.**

# Things to Come

In the first ten days of this book, we looked at prophecies of the Messiah. These Old Testament passages tell us who Jesus is and what He came to do on earth. Seeing prophecy fulfilled helps us trust that God's Word is divinely inspired (see 2 Tim. 3:16) and reminds us of God's faithfulness—He keeps every promise He makes.

While we covered many of the Old Testament prophecies during those ten days, we'll take a deeper look here into how Jesus fulfilled each one. The prophecy is filled in for you in the left column. Use the Scripture references in the right column to help you summarize how Jesus fulfilled each one.

| Prophecy | Fulfillment |
|---|---|
| **Genesis 3:15** The woman's offspring would strike the head of the serpent; the serpent would bruise his heel. | **Galatians 4:4; Hebrews 2:14** SUMMARY: |
| **Genesis 12:3; 22:18** All people through all generations would be blessed through Abraham's offspring. | **Matthew 1:1; Galatians 3:8,16; Hebrews 6:14** SUMMARY: |
| **Genesis 49:10** Jesus—the Messiah—would come from the line of Judah. | **Revelation 5:5** SUMMARY: |
| **Isaiah 52:13-53:12** Jesus would be despised and rejected. | **Matthew 8:17; 27:1-2,12-14,38** SUMMARY: |

| Prophecy | Fulfillment |
| --- | --- |
| **Isaiah 40:3-5**<br>Jesus—the Messiah—would free the oppressed, give sight to the blind, and share the good news. | **Matthew 3:3; Mark 1:3; Luke 3:4-5; John 1:23**<br>SUMMARY: |
| **Isaiah 40:10-11**<br>Jesus—the Messiah—would be the Good Shepherd who gave His life for His sheep. | **John 10:11; Hebrews 13:20; 1 Peter 2:24-25**<br>SUMMARY: |

Still, there are some prophecies about Jesus that remain to be fulfilled. Check out each of the following and summarize what we're waiting for.

**Isaiah 32:1-4 | Revelation 19:16; 20:6 —**

**Zechariah 2:10-13 | Revelation 5:13; 6:9; 21:24; 22:1-5 —**

As you finish writing your answers, consider how the earlier fulfillment of prophecies can help you keep faith in the things to come.

Chart adapted from Ralph P. Martin, "Messiah," ed. Chad Brand et al., *Holman Illustrated Bible Dictionary* (Nashville, TN: Holman Bible Publishers, 2003), 1112–1114.

# A Holy Hush

The month leading up to Christmas is often filled with excitement. Ugly sweater parties. Cookie exchanges. Cheesy holiday rom-coms. The list of activities seems endless. This season can be more than a marathon of madness, though; it can be a pause—a time when a holy hush falls on the world as we focus on what makes this season so special: Jesus, God in the flesh, came into the world to save us.

Celebrating Advent can help. Advent is a time of remembrance that has been observed by Christians throughout history. It begins on the fourth Sunday before Christmas and ends on Christmas day, and each of the four weeks focuses on a different theme: hope, peace, joy, and love.

For each week, choose an item from the meditate section, then choose an idea from the reflect section to help you focus on how it connects to Jesus and you!

## MEDITATE

### Week 1 Hope

**Psalm 119:14 ✦ John 1:9 ✦ Romans 5:5 ✦ Romans 15:13**
**Ephesians 1:18 ✦ 1 Peter 1:3 ✦ Hebrews 10:23**

QUOTE: "It is only when everything is hopeless that hope begins to be a strength at all."[1] — G. K. Chesterton

SONG: "Rescue" by Lauren Daigle

### Week 2 Peace

**Isaiah 9:6 ✦ Isaiah 52:7 ✦ Matthew 5:9 ✦ Matthew 5:23-24**
**John 14:27 ✦ Romans 5:1 ✦ Ephesians 4:32**

QUOTE: "God cannot give us a happiness and peace apart from Himself, because it is not there. There is no such thing."[2] — C.S. Lewis

SONG: "The War Is Over" by Bethel Music and Kalley Heiligenthal

**Week 3** Joy

**Zephaniah 3:17 + Psalm 16:11 + Psalm 40:3 + Psalm 51:12**
**Proverbs 17:22 + John 16:22 + Galatians 5:22**

QUOTE: "Those who know where the treasure lies joyfully abandon everything else to secure it."[3] —D.A. Carson

SONG: "Joy of the Lord" by Maverick City Music

**Week 4** Love

**Ezekiel 34:15-16 + Lamentations 3:31-33 + John 3:16**
**1 Corinthians 13:13 + Ephesians 4:2-3 + Colossians 3:14 + 1 John 4:10**

QUOTE: "Life is too short, the world is too big, and God's love is too great to live ordinary."[4] —Christine Caine

SONG: "Driven by Love" by Lindy Cofer & Circuit Rider Music

## REFLECT

- Write in a journal, or make a voice recording, describing your feelings when you read this verse or quote or listen to this song.
- Choose a Christmas-themed photo to post on social media along with a caption that includes your verse, the quote, or a lyric from the song. Include your reaction as well.
- Share your verse, the quote, or the song with a friend.
- Write your verse, the quote, or a lyric from the song on a slip of paper. Fold it and put it in a jar. Add to the jar from time to time, and draw slips of paper from it throughout the year to help you focus on Jesus.
- Create a poem or song based on the verse, quote, or song.

1. Gilbert K. Chesterton, *Heretics* (New York, John Lane Company: 1905), 119.
2. C.S. Lewis, *Mere Christianity* (New York: Macmillan, 1952), 53-54.
3. D. A. Carson, *Matthew,* The Expositor's Bible Commentary (Grand Rapids, MI: Zondervan Academic, 1984), 328.
4. Christine Caine, Twitter post, June 26, 2015, 12:00 p.m., https://twitter.com/ChristineCaine/status/614463191511240704.